FOOTBALL
STAR POWER

# Driving Force

## Jonny Zucker

Illustrated by Jacopo Camagni

EDGE

First published in 2014
by Franklin Watts

Text © Jonny Zucker 2014
Illustrations by Jacopo Camagni © Franklin Watts 2014
Cover design by Peter Scoulding

Franklin Watts
338 Euston Road
London NW1 3BH

Franklin Watts Australia
Level 17/207 Kent Street
Sydney, NSW 2000

A CIP catalogue record for this book
is available from the British Library.

(pb) ISBN: 978 1 4451 2617 3
(ebook) ISBN: 978 1 4451 2621 0
(Library ebook) ISBN: 978 1 4451 2625 8

1  3  5  7  9  10  8  6  4  2

Printed and bound by CPI Group (UK) Ltd, Croydon, CR0 4YY

Franklin Watts is a division of Hachette Children's Books,
an Hachette UK company.
www.hachette.co.uk

# CONTENTS

# CHAPTER 1
## STARTING AN ATTACK

"Mum," said Leo Diamond into his phone. "I'm going to be a bit late today. We're having a game of footie in the park."

It was 4 pm, and a group of sixteen kids from Leo's school had gathered on the hard football court in the local park.

"No problem," replied his mum, "but don't be too late. I've got pizza for supper."

"Nice one," said Leo. "I'll be back at about six thirty."

Leo ended the call and was putting his phone into his school bag when he felt a presence beside him. He looked round and there was the smug, smiling face of Gavin Mathers — the king of wind-ups.

"Was that Mummy on the phone?" asked Gavin in a baby voice. "Did you have to get her permission to stay out late?"

"Go away, Gavin!" snapped Leo, his body bristling with tension.

"Oh dear, have I upset baby?"

"I said, clear off!"

"Fine," nodded Gavin, reverting to his normal voice. "But let's see if you're a baby on the pitch as well." He strolled off.

"What was all that about?" asked Leo's best friend, Mac, walking over and seeing the hot and angry expression on Leo's face.

"It was just Gavin being...Gavin," said Leo through gritted teeth.

"Forget him," said Mac, "the guy is a grade one loser."

The kids formed themselves into two teams of eight. Mac and Gavin were on one side; Leo was on the other. Mac grinned at Leo when the teams were chosen; Gavin scowled at him.

The players were pretty evenly matched. Like Leo and Mac, everyone was in the school's first-team squad and most of them had played at least once for the team that season. Unfortunately Leo wasn't one of them. He was desperate for an appearance.

The game kicked off.

Leo was playing in central midfield, but while he wanted to attack, he found he was spending most of his time in defence. Defending was fine, but Leo preferred an attacking role, where he could make assists and score goals.

After fifteen minutes without many shots on goal, Mac hit a thunderous volley that bounced off the post and flew back towards Leo.

At last — a chance to get forward!

Leo controlled the ball on his chest, brought it down and started running up the pitch.

He increased his speed, hoping that his team-mates would join him, but most of them hung back. They were wary of the opposition hitting them with a counter-attack if Leo lost possession of the ball. One exception was a kid called Charlie on the left wing. Leo hit the ball to him, but Charlie spun round and passed the ball back into their own half.

Leo groaned as the ball rolled back to his keeper.

How were his team ever going to score if they weren't prepared to attack? How could he drive them on?

"Great leadership skills!" laughed Gavin, strutting over to Leo. "You really took your team with you then!"

"Don't be ridiculous!" snapped Mac, joining them. "Someone's got to start an attack for their team. At least Leo had a go. You've done next to nothing so far."

Gavin gave Mac a sour look and trotted back to his own half.

"Cheers," smiled Leo. "If you hadn't come over then I might have flattened him."

They both laughed and went back to join the game.

When the match was over and everyone else had drifted off, Leo and Mac sat on a fence, having a drink from their bottles of water, and talking.

"It would have been great if Gavin hadn't been here," muttered Leo.

"I totally agree," replied Mac. "But he goes to our school, he's friendly with the kids we know and he's in the first-team squad with us."

"I know," sighed Leo. "If only we could vaporise him. It would be brilliant to never hear his voice again."

"Come on," said Mac, standing up. "Let's go."

Leo stood too.

They walked out of the park, turned left and headed home.

## CHAPTER 2
## SELF COACHING

Leo was quiet and subdued when he got home. He ate supper with his mum, barely saying a word. After he'd helped her clear up, he went straight to his room. He was lying on his bed reading a football magazine, trying not to think about Gavin Mathers, when his mum put her head round the door.

"Is everything OK?" she asked.

Leo shrugged his shoulders. She came in and sat down on the edge of his bed.

"You know you can tell me anything," she said kindly. "If you want to talk, I'm listening."

Leo closed his magazine, took in a deep breath and blew it out.

"It's...it's just that sometimes I miss having Dad around." He felt guilty saying it, but it was the truth. He'd been thinking about him quite a lot recently.

"Of course you do," said Mum. "Every boy wants his dad."

"I know he walked out on us and I'm really angry about that, but we did have some good times, like kicking a ball around in the park. He taught me things about football; things I don't learn at school."

Mr Cross, who took the team at school, was an OK coach — he tried hard — but just didn't have the right skills.

"I could get you some private coaching sessions, if that's what you want?"

"No way," said Leo, who would have loved that, but knew how tight money was.

"I'd offer to coach you myself, but I don't think we'd get very far," smiled his mum. "Especially as you know ten times more about the game than me."

Leo grinned and made a decision. Dad wasn't coming back, and if he wasn't going to receive any extra coaching, the only way to improve would be to coach himself. He'd spend time practising his skills and studying the great players.

This thought lifted his spirits as he said goodnight to his mum. He lay awake thinking about the day ahead, before falling into a deep sleep.

There was no hard-court game after

school the next day, so Leo went to the park. He was intending to practise his skills and begin his self-coaching programme, but all the goals were in use. A group of young kids was being trained by two shaven-headed guys carrying whistles. Leo dropped his football and sat down on a bench.

The coaches clearly knew what they were doing, and the kids seemed to be having a great time. A wistful pang hit Leo. Would he be a better player if his dad was still around? Might his dad have started to coach him properly when he started secondary school? And what about a session with a professional coach? Could an hour or two with someone like that make a massive difference to his game?

Leo snapped out of his thoughts and pulled his football magazine from his bag. There was a smiling photo of Liverpool's Steven Gerrard on the front. A second later a blast of wind rushed across the park and swirled all around Leo. His face stung. His skin felt electric. He closed his eyes tightly.

# CHAPTER 3
## MIDFIELD MASTERCLASS

When Leo opened his eyes, he found himself standing in a street with lots of tightly packed red-brick houses. Turning to his right he saw a gigantic football stadium towering over him. He recognised it from pictures he'd seen. It was Anfield — Liverpool's stadium.

He turned to his left and saw a figure striding round the corner towards him.

It was Steven Gerrard!

Leo blinked in shock as Gerrard approached him and held out his hand. Leo shook Gerrard's hand, his feet rooted to the spot in amazement.

"All right?" nodded Gerrard.

Leo nodded back.

"I hear you're interested in getting some tips about playing in the centre-midfield position," said Gerrard.

"Y...y...yes," replied Leo, realising instantly that this was the real Gerrard, and not some computer game avatar. How did Gerrard know about his football aspirations? How had Leo got here?

"Well, don't expect a magic pill," said Gerrard. "I started early, but it took me a pretty long time to make it."

"How did you begin?" asked Leo, incredibly excited to be in the presence of the Liverpool and England legend.

"I'm from a place called Whiston, it's not too far from here," replied Gerrard. "Whiston Juniors was my first team. I loved it all: the training, learning new skills, the bonds that grew between the players."

"How old were you when you started at Liverpool?"

"They scouted me when I was playing for Whiston. I joined the Liverpool academy when I was nine. It was a big step up. Now I was being trained by professional coaches!"

"Did you stick out as a great player even then?"

"Not at all," said Gerrard. "There were loads of good players — kids who were faster, better passers and finishers than me. I knew I had to work really hard just to get to the same level as them."

"So you stuck with Liverpool the whole way through?" asked Leo.

Gerrard shook his head. "I'd been with the Liverpool academy for five years when I decided the club weren't taking enough notice of me. So around the age of fourteen, I started having trials at other clubs."

"Did that work?"

"I think the one that helped me most was Manchester United," laughed

Gerrard. "You know that Liverpool and Man United are bitter rivals. The coaches at Liverpool didn't like me going over there — they didn't want to see me playing for United. So they started focusing on me, telling me I was a Liverpool lad and that my future lay at Anfield, not Old Trafford."

"So they signed you up?"

"A few months after my seventeenth birthday, I became a Liverpool player, and a year or so later I played in my first Premier League game. It was Liverpool vs Blackburn Rovers. I was a last minute substitute, but I'm telling you, that minute was one of the greatest of my life."

"That's amazing," said Leo. "I'm in my school's first team squad, but as yet no scouts have been round to check us out."

"Sometimes they don't, and you have to approach them," said Gerrard. "But for the time being, let's not worry about scouts. Let's give you some football pointers."

"What...you're going to show me stuff?" mouthed Leo in astonishment.

"Absolutely," nodded Gerrard. "And that's why this will come in handy."

He produced a key from his pocket and they started walking towards the stadium.

A minute later, they were standing outside a narrow black gate. Gerrard inserted the key in the lock, turned it and the gate swung open. They walked through, the gate closing behind them.

"Welcome to Anfield," said Gerrard
with a grin. Shortly after, he led
Leo out onto the immaculate, lush
green pitch.

# CHAPTER 4
## ATTACKING PLAY

"OK," said Gerrard when they were on the pitch. "The first requirement of a great central midfielder is stamina. You've got to be prepared to get back and shield the defence, and go up to support the attack. You have to be a box-to-box player — think of Mario Götze and Thomas Müller. Those types of player sometimes win games almost entirely by themselves. They're not flash, but they're incredibly effective. A large part of their skill is their ability to cover huge sections of the pitch. So the first thing we're going to do is some running."

Leo drank in every word. This was

out of orbit!

Gerrard placed two white cones about thirty metres apart and he and Leo started sprinting and then jogging

and then sprinting between them. It was draining, brutal work, but Leo was fit and he could take it.

"The second skill is making surging runs," declared Gerrard. "You don't have to be flash, you don't have to use Ronaldo tricks and flicks, you just have to pound forward with the ball. This inspires everyone around you to move at pace to the opposition goal. If you play this way you'll be providing assists, as well as scoring goals. And that's one of the greatest things about playing in this position. You end up making vital tackles in your own half one minute, and the next minute find yourself in the opposite penalty area leaping for a header. It's the variety that makes it all so exciting."

For the next half hour Gerrard got Leo running with the ball between the cones, as fast and as powerfully as he could. He didn't try any fancy moves, he just ran at speed with the ball at his feet.

"Good work," said Gerrard. "The third skill is leadership. Even if you're not club captain, central midfielders must inspire those around them. Players like Juan Mata and Mathieu Flamini have totally got this. They read the game and yell at others to perform their roles. Players like this are vital. They're the engine room of a team."

"So what are we doing now?" asked Leo, aware that there weren't any other players around for him to shout at.

"You're going to run down the centre

of the pitch and I'm going to be on the left, the right or behind you. I'll keep switching positions. You need to be aware of where I am and play a one-two with me, telling me when you want the ball back. Got it?"

Leo nodded.

They walked to the centre circle and faced the "Kop" end of the stadium.

"OK, Leo," nodded Gerrard. "Let's go."

For the next forty minutes they practised, Leo racing forward with the ball, Gerrard popping up in all sorts of positions. The first few times Leo's passes went amiss and his cries went unanswered, but from then on he struck the ball with accuracy, called out for Gerrard's return pass and then thumped the ball into the net.

After this, they stood together in the penalty area, Gerrard stretching his arms, Leo leaning back against a goalpost.

"So what are the three skills of a great attacking midfielder?" asked Gerrard.

"Box-to-box, surging runs, inspire your team," replied Leo.

"You've got it," grinned Gerrard. "I've played my entire career with those three things in mind, and I'm still learning every day. You get some of these kids coming through and you see them make a move and you think, that's pretty good. I'll try that next time I play."

Leo nodded, exhausted but delighted.

"Can you just get the ball out of the net?" asked Gerrard.

"Sure," nodded Leo. He walked towards the back of the net and crouched down to pick up the ball. When he turned round, Steven Gerrard had vanished.

# CHAPTER 5
## CRAZY STORY

A blast of air swept across the Anfield turf, and Leo staggered back. He closed his eyes, and when he opened them a second later, he was back on the park bench, holding his magazine. Had he blacked out, or did he really just have a coaching session from Steven Gerrard?

Leo stood up, shook his head and started walking towards one of the pitches that was now empty. It was time to put his training into practice.

\* \* \* \* \* \* \* \* \* \* \* \* \* \* \* \* \* \*

Back at home, Leo was eating supper with his mum in their small kitchen.

"Do you believe someone can be in two places at the same time?" Leo asked her.

"What, you mean like teleporting?"

"Kind of," replied Leo, who had thought about telling his mum what had happened, until he realised that he would sound crazy.

"Sounds like a science-fiction story," said his mum. "Why do you want to know? Are there any school lessons you want to disappear from?"

Leo laughed. "That would be good!" His mum gave him a funny look, but didn't say anything more as she could see that Leo wanted to move on and talk about other things.

# CHAPTER 6
## STUDYING SKILLS

Leo stayed late at school the next day.
He'd been distracted during his lessons,
going over everything that Gerrard
had told him: box-to-box, surging
runs, inspire your team. He went to
the library with the intention of doing
his homework, but as the place was
pretty empty and there was no one
else studying, he headed over to the
computers. He started searching on
the net for classic attacking midfield
players — players who could change
the course of a game with their own
dedication and determination.

Here was the massive Yaya Touré
driving on his team with his powerful

runs and excellent passing. As well as providing loads of assists, Touré could score over twenty goals in one season — an incredible tally for a midfielder.

There was Ramires, a star for both his team and Brazil. His build was far slighter than Touré's, but his influence was just as vital. Ramires's stamina was outstanding — he was a real box-to-box player who seemed to cover every single blade of grass.

And what about Aaron Ramsey? He'd suffered a terrible injury just as he was emerging as a true midfield star. But grit and determination had seen him through the recovery process and he'd come back stronger, notching up the winning goal for Arsenal in the FA Cup final against Hull City.

Leo was so engrossed in watching highlights of these players' careers, that he didn't hear footsteps approaching from behind. Two hands grabbed his chair and yanked it backwards.

Leo yelped out in shock as he tumbled back, but before he hit the ground the same hands pushed the chair forward until it smacked into the desk. Leo jumped up and came face-to-face with Gavin Mathers.

"What was that for?" shouted Leo, giving Gavin a shove in the chest.

"It was just a joke!" snapped Gavin. "I reckoned someone who spent so much time in the library needed a bit of a wake up. Anyway, what is it you're looking at?"

Leo reached for the mouse to minimise the screen, but Gavin snatched it out of his hand and sat down on the chair.

"Best attacking central midfielders, eh?" said Gavin, looking at the screen. "Are you trying to become a better player by looking at all of these and studying their techniques?"

Gavin's voice was laced with a heavy dose of sarcasm.

"Get lost, Gavin!" snapped Leo angrily.

"Fine," replied Gavin, standing up. "But let me offer you one piece of advice."

Leo stared at him sullenly.

"Watching those guys won't help you a bit. To play like that you have to be blessed with natural talent. I, of course, have that in buckets, while you...well, let's put it this way: you're never going to be even a half-decent player."

And with that, Gavin strolled off, looking around the library and nodding at things as if he owned the place.

Leo tried hard to not let Gavin's words get to him, but it was no good.

The guy was a total ball of irritation, and Leo wished he'd just move to another school and get off his case.

Leo sat down and turned back towards the screen. His eyes picked out a photo of some Liverpool players in their red shirts. A buzzing noise filled his ears and the world around him went blurry.

He closed his eyes. When he opened them the library was gone. Instead, he was standing in the Liverpool football team changing room. The players sat on benches and in an instant, Leo could tell that there was serious tension in the air. In fact, the tension was so great, it felt as if the entire world had ended.

# CHAPTER 7
## PLAY LIKE WARRIORS

Leo was staring at the players. They looked stunned — completely defeated and dejected. He immediately spotted Steven Gerrard, but there were a few other faces he knew; Xabi Alonso from Spain was there, as was German international, Dietmar Hamann, and Polish goalkeeper, Jerzy Dudek. A date was written on a whiteboard in the corner of the room:

## 25th May 2005

The only player to have any kind of optimism or belief on their face was Gerrard. He beckoned to Leo.

Leo walked over and sat down in the space next to Gerrard; it was clear that the Liverpool captain was the only one who could see him.

A short man dressed in a dark blue suit, with a goatee beard, was standing and addressing the players. His face was red and he looked exhausted, but there was a gleam in his eye. It was Rafael Benítez, Liverpool's manager.

"OK, lads," said Benítez. "We're 3—0 down at half-time in the European Champions League final. Milan have played us off the park. Their shooting and passing have put us in the shade. It's not a good place to be."

Several of the players nodded, their heads hanging down in shame.

"But football as they say," went on

Benítez, "is a game of two halves, and from this second things are going to change for us."

"How are we going to turn this one round?" asked Hamann.

"We're going to play without fear," said Gerrard. "We're going to treat the game as if the first half never happened."

"Exactly!" nodded Benítez. "They scored a goal in the first fifty seconds — an act that would stun any team. But that's history now. Many teams have fought back from this sort of score and won in the end."

The players' faces filled with doubt.

"The boss is right," said Gerrard. "And if we're not going to do it for ourselves, then we have to do it for the fans. Some of them have saved up for this trip for months. If we don't fight back we'll be letting all of them down."

A few heads went up after this comment as the players remembered they were carrying the hopes of thousands of Liverpool supporters, not just in Istanbul's Atatürk stadium, but for all Reds' fans across the globe.

"By keeping possession of the ball and making each pass count, we CAN do this!" declared Benítez. "But every single one of you must be focused. No fear, no excuses."

Suddenly each player's head was up and looking at Benítez.

"We play like warriors!" exclaimed Gerrard, jumping to his feet. "We show Milan the spirit and strength we have in reserve. We take the game to them and we give them the shock of their lives."

In a second, all of the other players had stood up too and a loud chorus of "YES!" rang around the changing room.

Inspire your team.

That's what Gerrard and Benítez had just done between them.

Leo got off the bench as the players stepped out into the corridor. It was time for the second half.

Gerrard put his hand on Leo's

shoulder. "This is your moment," said Gerrard. "You're going to be the engine that drives this team forward."

And with that Gerrard stepped forward, leaving an outline of his body.

"Me?" gasped Leo.

"There's no time for waiting," said Gerrard sternly. "The whistle will be going soon."

Leo gulped nervously, nodded and stepped into Gerrard's outline. Gerrard winked at him and they hurried out into the cauldron of noise and colour that was the Atatürk stadium. Gerrard stood on the touchline, while a very nervous Leo took a deep breath and ran onto the pitch.

# CHAPTER 8
## INSPIRING GOAL

Before Leo had any further time to think, the ref's whistle blew and the second half was under way. As he ran towards the action he couldn't help thinking that coming back from 3–0 down in a game this big would be something of a miracle.

Gerrard's words from Anfield zipped through his brain. "Box-to-box, surging runs, inspire your team."

Leo took these words to heart. He got stuck in immediately, passing, tackling and harrying opponents in different sections of the pitch. He felt adrenaline surging through his body and a sensation of incredible determination. He was playing in both boxes with the energy of three players.

When John Arne Riise got the ball on the left wing, twenty yards from the penalty area, Leo knew what he had to do. Racing into the penalty area he watched as Riise's cross floated into the box.

Leo had his face to the ball, and as it flew through the air, he leaped off the

ground, twisted his body to the right and smashed in an incredibly powerful header. Dida in the Milan goal dived for it, but its force was too strong.

Milan 3 – Liverpool 1.

As Leo ran back towards the centre circle, with his team-mates pursuing him, he remembered what Gerrard had told him about bringing the fans with you. So he raised both arms in the air and threw his hands up and down, challenging them to reach even higher levels of support. The response was immediate. The red half of the stadium had already been going crazy over Leo's goal, but now he had motioned to them, they went even madder and louder.

"Even though we're still way behind,

we must be in with a chance now,"
thought Leo.

From the Milan kickoff, Leo played
like a man possessed. Yelling at team-
mates to cover Milan players, his
passes were accurate and urgent, and
four minutes later, Liverpool's attack
built up again.

After a series of neat passes,
Liverpool's Vladimír Šmicer received
the ball just outside Milan's D.
Thumping a mighty shot, the ball
curled towards the left-hand side of
goal and despite goalkeeper Dida's
desperate lunge, it eluded him and
smashed into the back of the net.

Milan 3 — Liverpool 2.

Leo joined in the team's celebrations
but within seconds he was yelling

at everyone to get back into their positions.

"We're not even drawing yet,"

shouted Leo, "let alone winning!" He had to inspire them to keep going and focus on the task in hand.

And then Leo looked at the expressions on the faces of the Milan players. He felt a cold pulse of fear.

That was because the Milan players were furious; furious with themselves. To go from 3—0 up to 3—2 was verging on disaster. Suddenly they looked like a bunch of angry dinosaurs whose sole aim in life was to crush anyone standing in their way.

The fightback had been amazing so far, but would Milan's steely resolve now extend their lead and take the game beyond Liverpool's reach?

# CHAPTER 9
## IMPOSSIBLE TO BELIEVE

Very shortly after Milan's kickoff another opportunity presented itself.

Leo got the ball in the Milan half and went on a surging run. Other Liverpool players were shouting for the ball, but Leo was totally fixed on route one — straight into the Milan penalty area. As he charged inside, with four Milan players around him, Gattuso made a lunge for the ball and tripped Leo up. He crashed to the floor and heard the referee instantly blowing for a penalty.

The Milan defenders were distraught and crowded round the ref, screaming that there had only been minimal contact and that Leo had dived. But

the ref shooed them away and kept
pointing to the spot.

Leo got up, his heart pumping
wildly in his chest, his hands hot and
sticky. He was delighted he had won a
penalty, but would he be the one who
had to take it? Scoring penalties in
the playground or the park was fine,
but to take a real one, in a match
this important, when the penalty spot
looked like it was miles away from the
goal. That was an entirely different
thing.

But Xabi Alonso was already picking
up the ball and placing it on the penalty
spot. The Milan players finally left the
referee alone and they, along with the
Liverpool players, stood on the edge of
the penalty area and watched.

The Milan fans shrieked to put Alonso off, while the Liverpool fans fell into a hushed silence, some unable to look.

It seemed like an age before the ref finally blew his whistle and Alonso ran up to strike the ball. It was a good shot with decent power and it hurtled to the left side of the goal. Dida chose the right direction and palmed the ball away with both hands. Leo felt a devastating shock in his body — Alonso's

penalty had been saved, but Alonso had other plans. He crashed forward and thumped in the rebound.

Milan 3 — Liverpool 3.

The Liverpool players mobbed Alonso for scoring, and Leo for getting the penalty. Liverpool had scored all three goals within fifteen minutes of the second half kicking off. It was an immense feat.

Leo had followed Gerrard's principles: box-to-box, surging runs, inspire your team.

The Milan players' faces were pale and shocked. How could they have given up a 3—0 lead? It was almost impossible to believe.

Leo ran towards the Liverpool fans, punching the air and screaming with delight. The fans were delirious. Never before had such pessimism turned to such optimism.

Leo knew the game wasn't over. There was still half an hour to play. But he was amazingly proud of his role in this reversal. He had stuck to Gerrard's guiding words and driven the team forward.

He was waiting for the Milan kick-off when he saw Gerrard motioning to him from the Liverpool bench. Leo ran over and saw a smile of total joy on Gerrard's face.

"Fifteen minutes!" cried Gerrard, putting an arm round Leo's shoulder. "Fifteen minutes to get three goals back, and you were in the thick of it!"

Leo beamed and Gerrard released him.

"You've done magnificently, Leo, but

I'm going to take things from here, OK?"

One half of Leo was crushed; he desperately wanted to carry on playing in this remarkable game. But the other half knew he had experienced the most incredible quarter of an hour of a lifetime, and that none of it would have happened without Steven Gerrard. So he nodded and stepped out of Gerrard's outline. Gerrard climbed back in and ran straight towards the centre circle, clapping his team-mates and shouting out instructions.

Leo was eager to watch the rest of the game, but the high-pitched buzzing sounded again, his surroundings went blurry, and a split second later he was back in the school library.

# CHAPTER 10
## DRIVING THE ATTACK

Leo's body was still tingling with excitement as he googled the 2005 Champions League Final in Turkey.

He read the match report with awe. After his surging fifteen minutes, the rest of the second half had been goalless. Kaka did have a good chance for Milan in the last minute, but he couldn't direct Japp Stam's header into the Liverpool goal.

There were few chances in extra time, and any that Milan had were saved by the outstanding Dudek.

So it went to penalties.

Milan failed to score with their first two and at 3–2 to Liverpool, Milan's

Shevchenko had to score for his team to remain in the final. The penalty was a central one and Dudek went right. However, kicking out his legs, the Liverpool keeper whacked the ball clean away.

The penalty shootout was over.

Liverpool had won the Champions League!

Leo grinned to himself. However weird it was to accept or believe, he had been part of that victory.

* * * * * * * * * * * * * * * * * *

The next day after school, Leo and Mac headed down to the local park in search of a good kickabout. It was a sunny afternoon and there were lots of people out walking their dogs or sitting on benches soaking up the rays. There were already some kids from school there, including Gavin. Leo groaned inside.

"Look out, it's the student of the year," called out Gavin. "He studies other footballers, but can't play himself."

A couple of people laughed, but most ignored this comment.

They quickly sorted out sides. Leo and Mac were on one team; Gavin would be facing them on the other. It was seven-a-side, and Leo opted to play in central midfield behind two strikers.

He would stick to Gerrard's three-point plan: box-to-box, surging runs, inspire your team.

In the first few minutes Leo saw little of the ball, but then he picked it up on the halfway line. The other two midfielders, boys called Dan and Kyle, were hovering, unsure of what he was going to do. Without hesitation Leo shouted, "Let's hit them!"

Dan and Kyle immediately followed Leo's instructions and started running.

Leo began a surging run, exchanging passes with Kyle, before bearing down on the opposing side's penalty area.

Gavin lunged in to try to take the ball off Leo, but Leo squared it to Dan and jumped over Gavin's outstretched legs. Gavin hit the turf with a resounding thud.

"NOW!" yelled Leo.

Dan crossed the ball over the

goalie's head. Leo took it on his chest, dummied a shot and passed to Kyle, who smacked a strong volley home.

"GOAL!" shouted Kyle, who ran over to Leo to exchange high-fives. It had been a beautiful move, and Leo had been the driving force behind the goal. He punched the air in delight.

"This isn't the Champion's League final!" snarled Gavin, dragging himself back to his feet.

"No," thought Leo, as he jogged back to the centre circle. "I've already played in one of those."

# FOOTBALL STAR POWER

**There are four books to collect!**

978 1 4451 2615 9 pb  978 1 4451 2619 7 ebook

**Free-kick Pro**
Jonny Zucker

978 1 4451 2616 6 pb  978 1 4451 2620 3 ebook

**Demon Dribbler**
Jonny Zucker

978 1 4451 2617 3 pb  978 1 4451 2621 0 ebook

**Driving Force**
Jonny Zucker

978 1 4451 2618 0 pb  978 1 4451 2622 7 ebook

**Hottest Shot**
Jonny Zucker